For Randi and Harper and everyone celebrating the magic of their "firsts."

www.iamkiaharris.com

ISBN 978-1-7342186-3-3

Text and illustrations copyright ©2020 by Taye Jones. All rights reserved.
Published by Kia Harris Juniors, an imprint of Kia Harris, LLC dba KH Publishers.

Illustrations by Dez Carter, Designs by Dez.

Printed in the U.S.A.

First Hardback Edition, September 2020

Liam's First Cut

Taye Jones

Illustrated by Dez Carter

It's Friday morning and Liam is excited! Tomorrow is a big day. On Saturday Liam and his Dad are going to the barbershop for the first time. Liam is going to get his first haircut.

Every week, Liam's Mom braids his hair while his Dad goes to the barbershop.

Liam has wanted to visit the barbershop with his Dad for a long time.

Now the big day is almost here! Liam is going to get his first cut at Mr. Jay's Barbershop.

Liam stares in the bathroom mirror holding his toothbrush and wonders what the barbershop will look like.

He wonders who will be there and what everyone will be doing.

"Maybe Juan will be there with his Tio," he thinks to himself. "Or maybe Jack and Uncle Carl will be there too!"

Suddenly Liam jumps when he hears a familiar voice. "Liam!!! Time for breakfast!" Mom yells from the kitchen.

Liam finishes brushing his teeth and puts on his clothes.

Morning Schedule!

- ☑ Wake up
- ☑ Make Bed
- ☑ Wash Face
- ☑ Brush Teeth
- ☑ Put on Clothes
- ☐ All Done

He checks the last box of his morning schedule. He grabs his backpack and goes downstairs to the kitchen.

With little time to spare, Liam takes a bagel to-go and kisses his Mom goodbye.
He and Dad head off to the bus stop. Liam doesn't want to miss his bus for school.

Liam rides the school bus and dreams some more about his big day tomorrow.

A buzzing bee flies into the window and buzzes near his ear.

He waves the bee away. "Will the barber's clippers sound like that?" he thinks. Liam starts to worry.

The bus arrives in front of PS#14, and Liam walks towards the front doors.

Liam sees Mr. Paul, the custodian cutting the grass.

Liam thinks of the clippers again and gets scared thinking about the noise that will be in his ears.

"Tomorrow, Dad is taking me to his special place. I'm going to get my first cut at Mr. Jay's Barbershop."

After school, Liam comes home and shows Mom the social story his teacher and therapist made to help him get ready for his special trip to the barbershop.

They go through the pages together and look at the photos to help Liam know what to expect.

That night Liam is so excited he can hardly sleep. He stares at the stars on his ceiling, waiting for morning to arrive.

He knows that soon he will finally be at the barbershop for his first cut!

Early the next morning, Dad calls out to Liam, "Rise and Shine, buddy! We have to get a move on."

...am hops out of bed and gets ready. ...am grabs his juice and kisses his Mom ...oodbye. He then heads off with Dad to ...r. Jay's Shop.

When they arrive at the shop, Liam pushes the door open. His ears are greeted with the sound of music playing and lots of talking.

He can hear men talking about sports. He sees a tall man sweeping puffs of hai from the floor.

He sees other men and boys waiting for their turns to get a cut, and he sees some Moms with their sons waiting too. "Hey there, little man," yells Mr. Jay. "We've been waiting for you. You're next!"

Liam and Dad sit near the window. Liam looks around Mr. Jay's shop. He doesn't see his friend Juan or his cousin Jack, but he sees Mr. Paul from school. He's playing a video game while waiting for his turn.

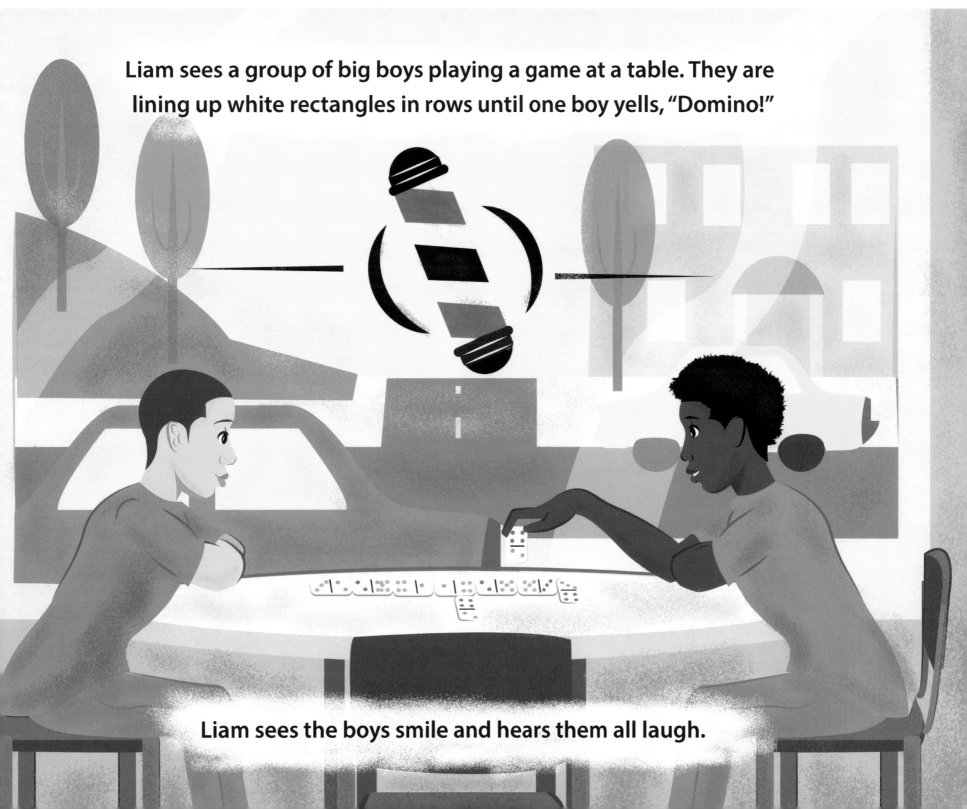

Liam sees a group of big boys playing a game at a table. They are lining up white rectangles in rows until one boy yells, "Domino!"

Liam sees the boys smile and hears them all laugh.

Mr. Jay spins the chair around, and Liam sees Uncle Carl. Mr. Jay sprays his hair and adds some powder to help brush away all the freshly cut hairs.

"Hi Uncle Carl!," Liam exclaims. "I'm getting a cut today too."

"That's right, little man, and it is your turn," says Mr. Jay.
Dad helps Liam into the big red chair. Mr. Jay spins him around to the mirror.

"So what are we doing today?" asks Mr. Jay. Dad replies, "Take it down, Mr. Jay– Liam' getting a fade today."

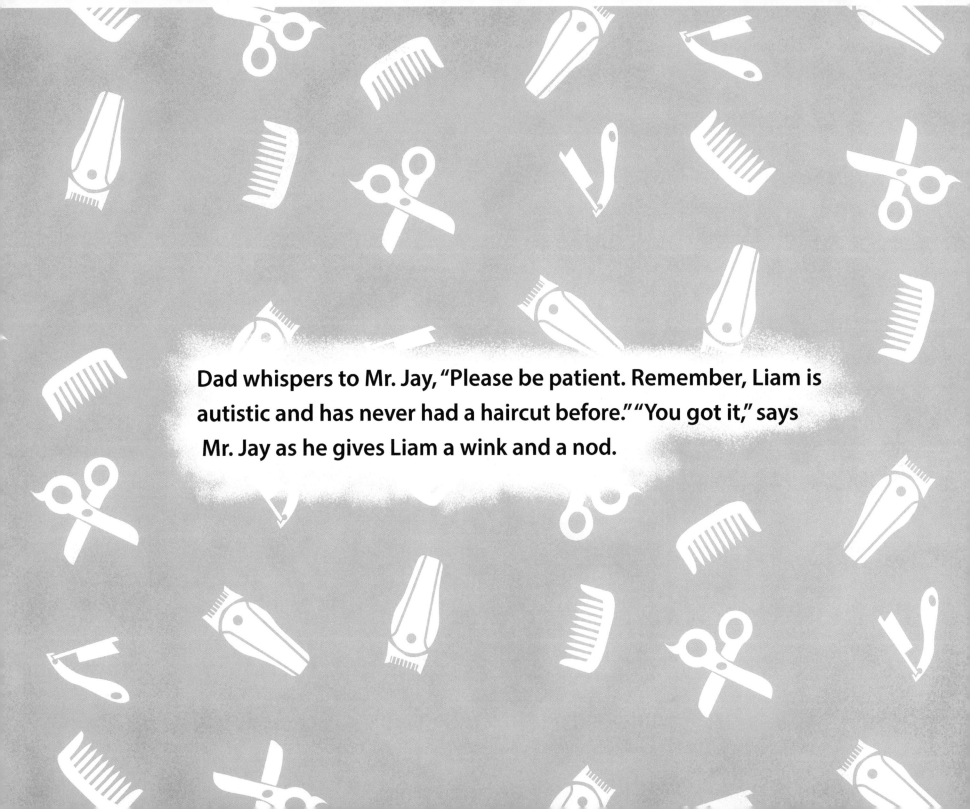

Dad whispers to Mr. Jay, "Please be patient. Remember, Liam is autistic and has never had a haircut before." "You got it," says Mr. Jay as he gives Liam a wink and a nod.

Mr. Jay pulls out a brand new blue cape and gives it a snap. Liam starts to get nervous as Mr. Jay places the cape over his chest and pulls out the clippers. "Don't worry, Liam. My cape will protect you - just like a superhero.

And the clippers may tickle a bit, but it won't hurt." Mr. Jay turns on the clippers and places the trimmer on Liam's arm. "How's that? See - it just hums and tickles." Liam laughs as the buzzing clipper tickles his arm.

Dad gives him a wink and asks, "Are you ready?" Liam nods and smiles. He takes a deep breath and remembers the photos in the story from his teacher.

Mr. Jay begins to cut. The clippers buzz lightly- even quieter than that buzzing bee or the lawnmower.

Liam closes his eyes and pretends the puffs of hair falling to the floor are cotton candy. The music coming out of the speakers drowns out the buzzing sounds of the clippers.

He opens his eyes again and imagines the man playing video games is a real basketball player running up and down the court. And he imagines the men across the room talking about sports are the TV announcers calling every play.

"Alright, Liam, my man. You are all done." Mr. Jay gives the chair a final spin.

The chair stops in front of the mirror, and Liam gets a look at his finished cut. "I like it! Thank you, Daddy! Thank you, Mr. Jay!"

Mr. Jay gives Liam a high-five and hands Dad a baggie filled with a few locks of hair as a keepsake.

"Now we have a reminder of the special day when you got your first cut." Says Dad. "I'll never forget this day and I will never forget my first cut!" Liams agrees.

Stay Connected with Taye Jones

Books signings, book readings, publicity, and media

Website: https://tayejones.com

Email: hello@tayejones.com

Professional and Therapy Services

Phone: 347.559.1517

Email: info@havingoursay.org

Website: www.havingoursay.org

Providing services to clients in the Northern NJ area

Affiliations

 - SMILES FOR SPEECH

 - AMERICAN SPEECH-LANGUAGE-HEARING ASSOCIATION (ASHA)

Shontaye Glover is an alumnus of Morgan State University in Baltimore, MD and received her masters of science degree in communication disorders from William Paterson University in New Jersey. She is a certified speech-language pathologist and Founder and CEO of Having Our Say, LLC where her private therapy practice focuses on evaluating and providing therapy to children with communication disorders. She also produces a blog for parents and caregivers providing tips and resources to help enhance language development in children.

Shontaye's dedication to children and children with special needs has a global reach as she serves as an executive board member for Smiles for Speech, Inc., a nonprofit organization that provides intervention and resources to children from disadvantaged communities across the globe. Through her efforts, she has supported Smiles for Speech with projects in Ghana and Kenya, Africa.

Shontaye's commitment to promoting language development through literacy and increasing diversity in children's literature has now led to the completion of her first literary work- "Liam's First Cut." Written under the pen name of "Taye Jones", Shontaye weaves together the beauty of fatherhood, community, and neurodiversity as Liam, a black boy diagnosed with autism, approaches a day he's been anticipating for quite some time. Liam takes us on a journey towards a big rite of passage in every boy's life and Taye gives us a glimpse at how Liam's preparation for visiting the barbershop may differ from others.

Taye lives in NJ with her family. When she's not writing, she enjoys eating pizza, running, listening to music, and spending time at the beach.

CPSIA information can be obtained at www.ICGtesting.com
Printed in the USA
LVIW011707090321
680992LV00007B/57
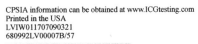